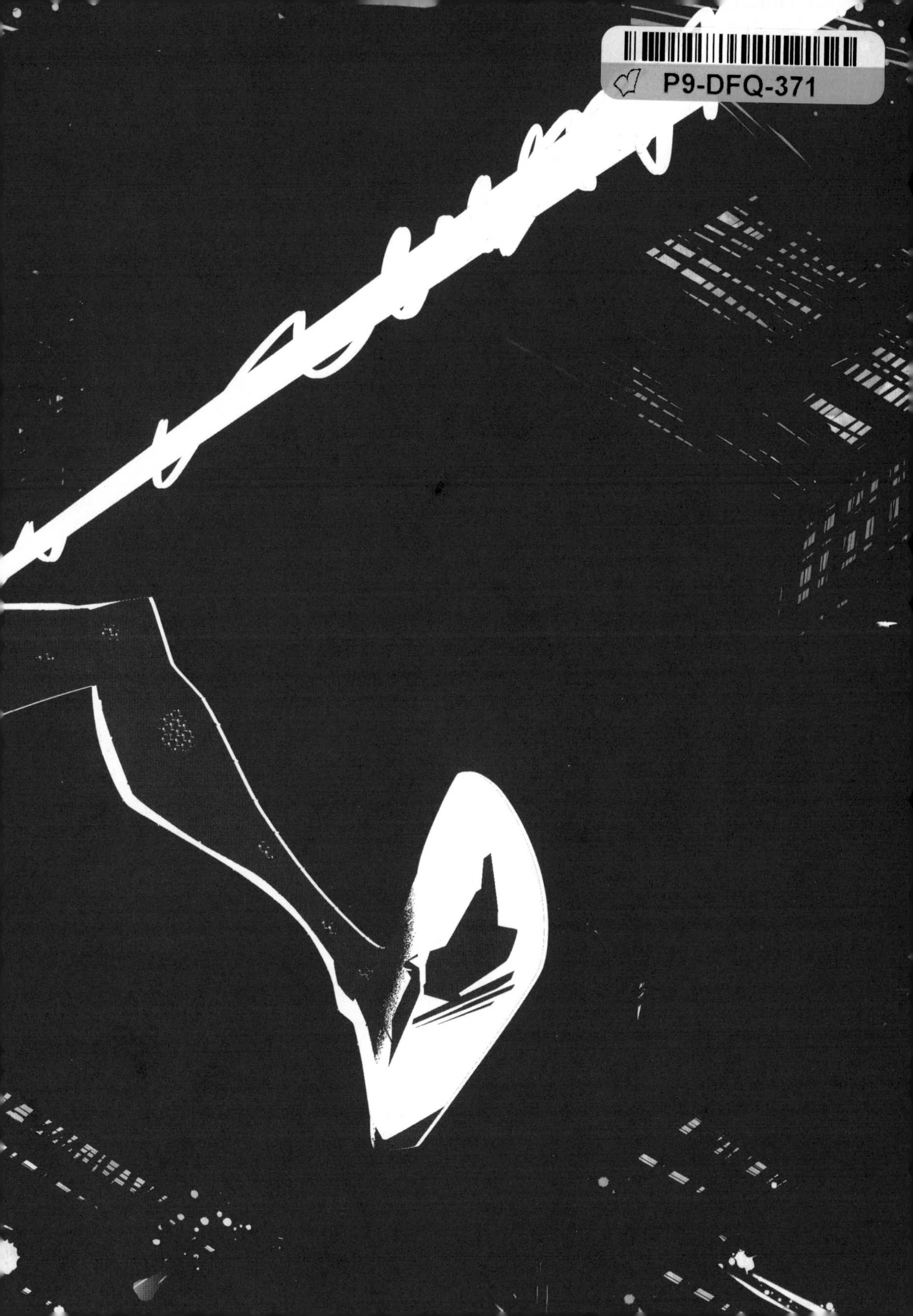

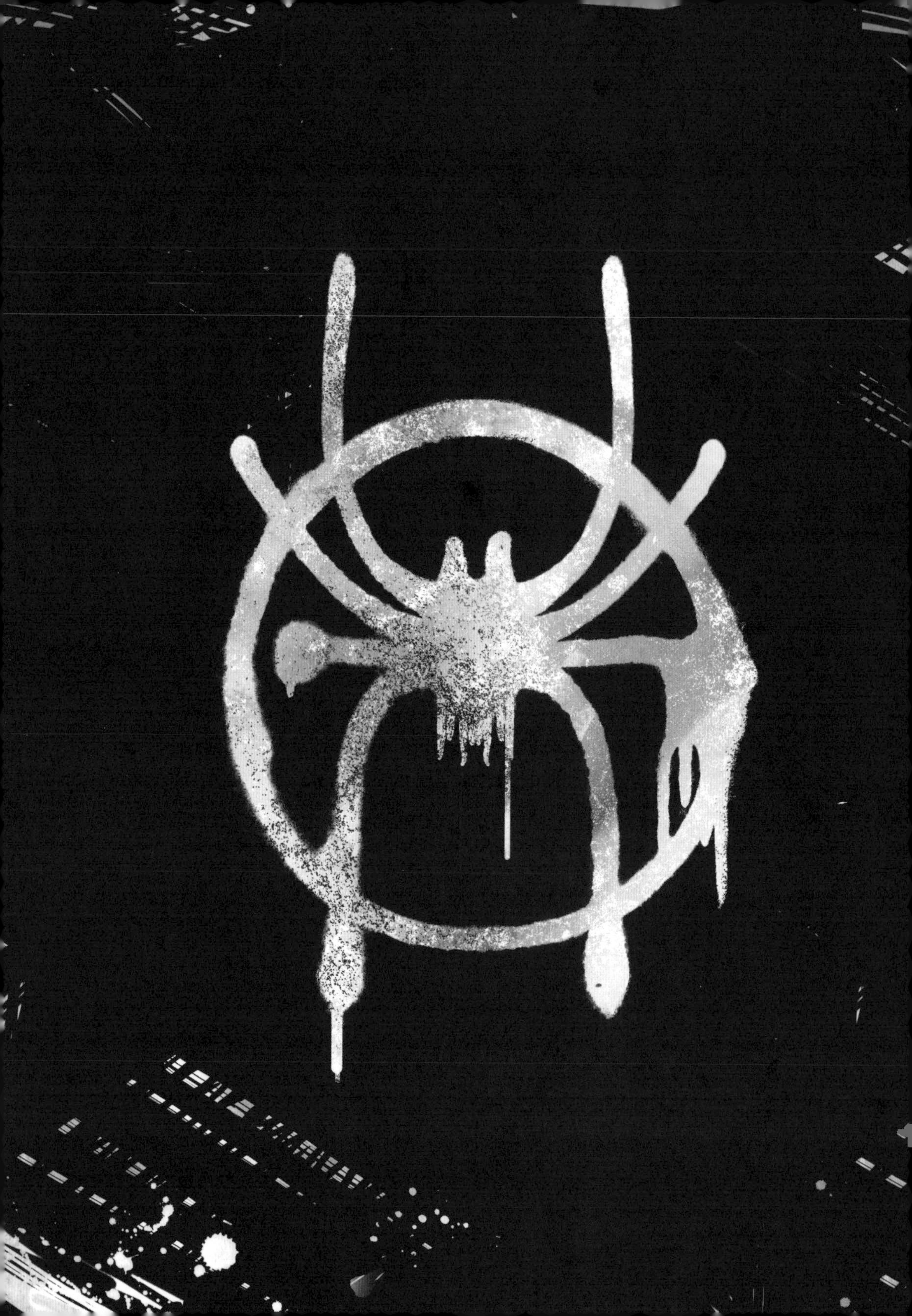

THIS JOURNAL BELONGS TO:

STOP!

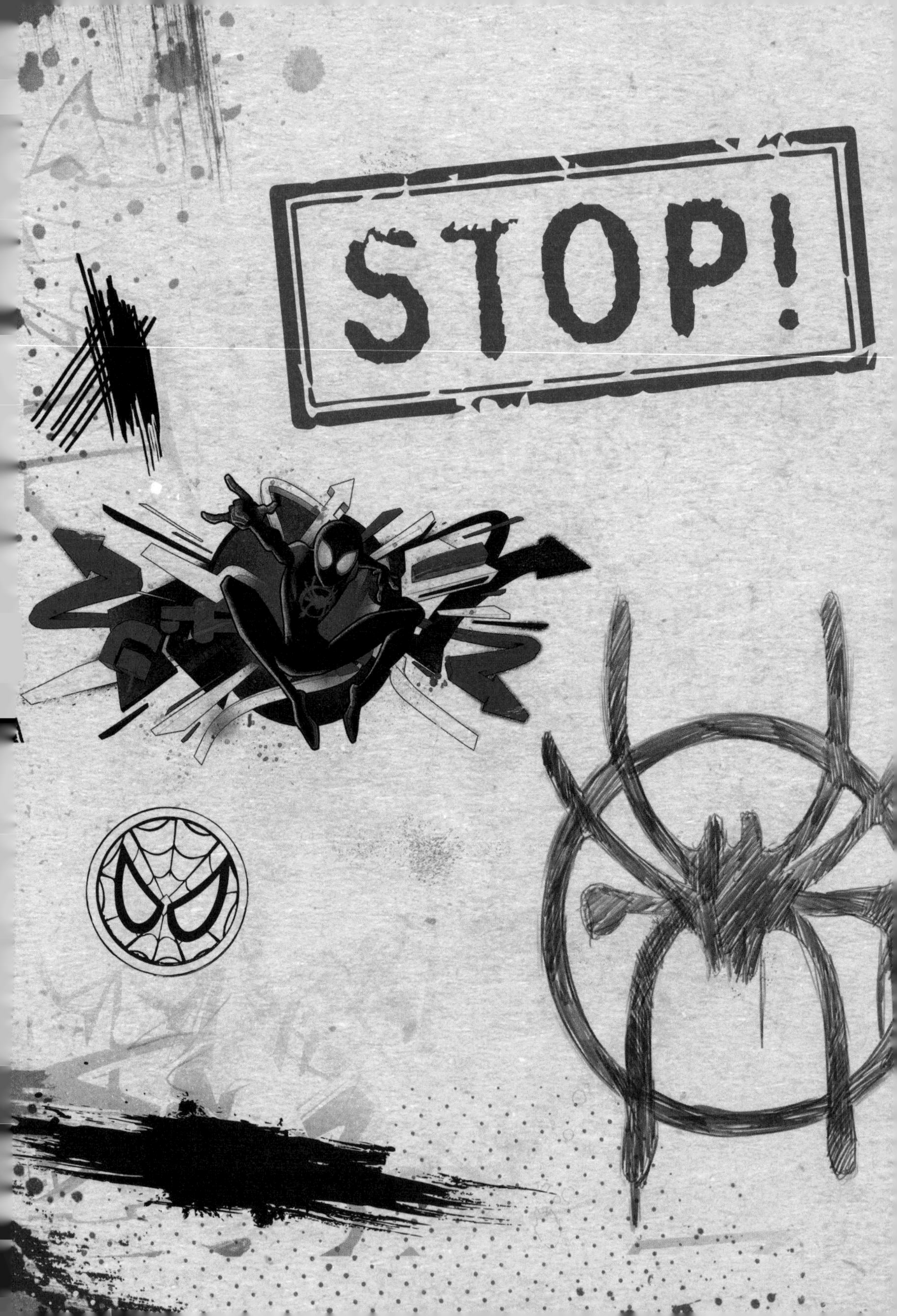

SPIDER-MAN

INTO THE SPIDER-VERSE

Hachette Book Group supports the right to free expression and the value of copyright. The purpose of copyright is to encourage writers and artists to produce the creative works that enrich our culture.

The scanning, uploading, and distribution of this book without permission is a theft of the author's intellectual property. If you would like permission to use material from the book (other than for review purposes), please contact permissions@hbgusa.com. Thank you for your support of the author's rights.

Little, Brown and Company
Hachette Book Group
1290 Avenue of the Americas, New York, NY 10104
Visit us at LBYR.com

First published as *Spider-Man: Into the Spider-Verse: The Journal*
by Centum Books Ltd in 2018 in Great Britain

First U.S. Edition: November 2018

Little, Brown and Company is a division of Hachette Book Group, Inc.
The Little, Brown name and logo are trademarks of Hachette Book Group, Inc.

The publisher is not responsible for websites (or their content) that are not owned by the publisher.

Library of Congress Control Number: 2018956525

ISBNs: 978-0-316-48041-3 (paper over board), 978-0-316-48036-9 (ebook),
978-0-316-48038-3 (ebook), 978-0-316-48037-6 (ebook)

Printed in the United States of America

LSC-k

SPIDER-MAN

INTO THE SPIDER-VERSE

Where I Belong

MILES TELLS HIS STORY, HIS WAY

Mom, Dad—if you're STILL reading this, then

STOP!

This is MY journal!

It's just going be a ton of boring science stuff.

Y'know, page after page of Multiverse Theory and what it means...

LITTLE, BROWN AND COMPANY
New York   Boston

Hey!

Okay, so it's been a wild time.

I think if I write down some of my thoughts, hopefully it'll help me to get a handle on thing

I wasn't joking when I said that I love scienc and Multiverse Theory and all that stuff. I d But lately, I kind of have some other interes Well, ONE other interest.

Have you ever heard of Spider-Man?

Of course you have

Well, funny thing...

I AM Spider-Mar

Well, one of 'em, anyway.

Confusing?

Yeah, I know how it feel But stick with me and we'll work it out.

This is my family.

Dad
(Jefferson)

Uncle Aaron
(uh, Uncle Aaron)

Mom
(Rio)

Me
(Miles, obvs)

Now, I (love) my parents.

My mom is cool and my dad is...well, he's cool, I guess.

But he's a police officer.

He's a "by the book" kind of guy.
And he sort of doesn't like Spider-Man. ←
The original one.

Oh yeah, and Uncle Aaron. I almost forgot about him.
He's my dad's brother. I like him a lot, but according
to my parents, he's kind of a bad influence.

Y'know, 'cause he likes to have FUN.

Wait, that's confusing, too. Well, I'll try to explain it later.

Here I am in school! Learning!
Getting smart(er)!

I was a <u>little nervous</u> about switching schools

(did I mention that I used to go to Brooklyn Middle School?)

and sometimes, if I'm being truthful,
I'd like to go back.

But Brooklyn Visions Academy...

WOW!

The teachers there are <u>amazing</u>,
and I can really learn a lot.

I really miss my old friends, though.
Maybe if I give these new kids a <u>chance</u>...?

SPIDEY

MORALES

One major downside to BVA—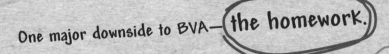the homework.

There's a ton of it.

Not that we didn't have a lot at Brooklyn Middle.

But I swear they hand out homework by the truckload here.

So here's a pic of me, drowning in math or whatever,

and that's Ganke.

I'll write more about him later.

Remember how I mentioned that my parents don't like me hanging out with Uncle Aaron?

Yeah, well, take a look at this pic.

This is probably what they're talking about.

LOL

We **don't** go out and get into **trouble** or anything, but Uncle Aaron sort of encourages me to head out and

express myself.

After we climb a really tall fence.

This is what I'm talking about!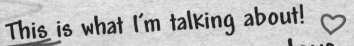

I love science and all, but I also **love** making art.

I'll sketch things during the day, then go out at night with Uncle Aaron to make these works of art on subway walls.

Uncle Aaron says my dad used to take him down here when they were younger.

Before he became a cop.

I like hanging out with Uncle Aaron,

because I can actually forget about everything else

and just concentrate on art.

It helps keep me focused.

Except for that one time when I went down there
and got bitten by this weird glowing spider.

That kind of unfocused everything really quickly.

So that's my life in a nutshell.

I have good parents,

go to a new school

that's NOT my old school,

have a...roommate who doesn't really talk to me,

and I was bitten by a spider.

That gave me powers.

Friends and Family

I talked a little about my mom and dad, and I sort of mentioned Ganke already. But I want to write more about them. So check out the next few pages!

DAD

MOM

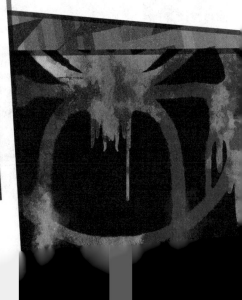

UNCLE AARON

GANKE

WANDA

So, yeah, Mom and Dad.

Rio and Jefferson.

Not that I'd ever call them that to their faces—not unless I felt like never leaving the house again for the rest of my life.

MOM

My mom <u>always</u> has my back, and I think we really get each other. At least, I feel like she gets me.

DAD

But my dad? Well...I know he wants what's best for me and I know he loves me, but... <u>he's just really hard on me.</u> Maybe one day things will be better between us.

Here's a selfie of me with Aaron Davis, my dad's brother and my uncle.

LEGEND.

My dad is always saying stuff to me like,

"u don't want to end up like your uncle Aaron, do you?"

or

"We all make choices in life, Miles— don't make choices like your uncle Aaron!"

Anyway,

I love Uncle Aaron, but he's kind of secretive sometimes.

Like, I don't know **what** he's got going on.

But there's **something.**

I really **loved** going to Brooklyn Middle School.

I had it all worked out, you know?

I could ace any test, breeze through my homework, and I had lots of friends.

Now that I'm going to Visions,

they like to give me a hard time, making fun of my school uniform.

I tell them that **Visions makes me wear it—** it's not my idea of fashion.

Not that I'm sure I really have any idea about fashion.

I grew up in a really great neighborhood.

Everyone knows everybody, and we're all pretty friendly with one another.

One of my neighbors, Herschel? He says **"hi"** to me every time I walk past his place.

"Buenas dias, Miles!"

Herschel says he likes to greet me that way because my mom is from Puerto Rico.

Which is pretty cool of him, even though I'm from Brooklyn.

The guy gets an A for effort!

Ganke is my roommate at Visions.

GANKE

ME

For the first couple of weeks, I wasn't sure if Ganke could talk or not.

All I knew about him was, he went to class, did his homework, and he liked to read Spider-Man comics with his headphones on.

But after a little while, we warmed up to each o

And then there's Wanda.

At least, she says her name is Wanda. Because when I first met her, she told me her name was Gwanda. **With a G.** And that she's South African but was raised in the States, which is why she doesn't have an accent. Turns out she was just messing with me.

That's how you start a beautiful friendship!

WANDA, AKA GWANDA

Yeah, right!

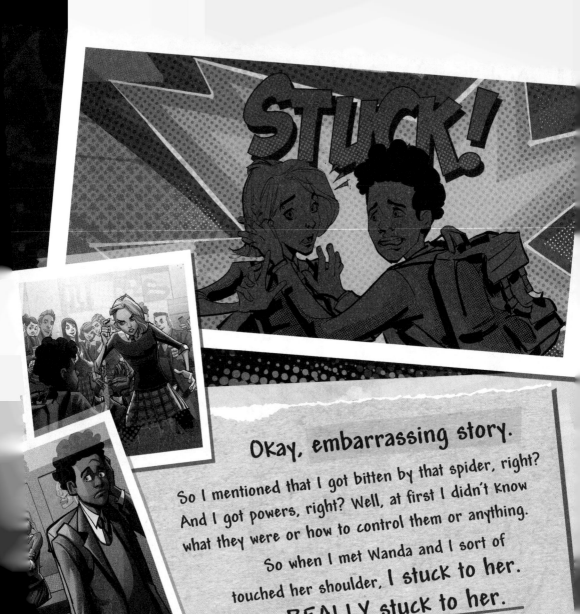

STUCK!

Okay, embarrassing story.

So I mentioned that I got bitten by that spider, right? And I got powers, right? Well, at first I didn't know what they were or how to control them or anything.

So when I met Wanda and I sort of touched her shoulder, **I stuck to her.** **Like, REALLY stuck to her.**

The more I tried to get unstuck, the **more** stuck I got, and then pretty soon her **hair** was involved. The school nurse **had to shave her hair** just to separate us.

EMBARRASSING.

Another (slightly less embarrassing) story?

So I sort of sneaked out of Visions Academy one night after I first got there, to go see Uncle Aaron.

I thought nobody saw me. **I thought wrong.**

The security guard, whose name is...

WOW, you know, I don't know what his name is.

Ooops Anyway.

He saw me the next day and ran after me. I tried to lose him and accidentally ran into his office.

That was a hot mess.

To be continued...

MILES MORALES

Made it in the end!

So, other than a **few** embarrassing incident
I'm a pretty lucky kid.

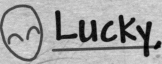 **Lucky.**

because I have
people in my life
who really care
about me.

And who like to wear headphones
and read Spider-Man comic books,
or tell me that their name is really Gwanda

Brooklyn Visions Academy

My new school!

I'm **still** trying to figure out where everything is, who everybody is, and...**well, everything!**

It's a big place, a lot bigger than Brooklyn Middle School.

You could easily get lost. **Let's hope I don't!***

*I DEFINITELY WILL.

I remember the **first time** I walked into the lobby of Visions Academy., **Everyone** seemed **taller** than me and all I could see were **blue uniforms everywhere.**

WOOSH!

At first, I thought the place was kind of elitist—y'know,

I just wanted to go back to Brooklyn Middle with my **normal** friends,

instead of a bunch of **overachieving brainiacs.**

But Mom and Dad (especially Dad)

wanted me to go here.

It **wasn't easy** getting into Visions Academy.

First, you had to win a lottery to even be considered for a spot.
Then, you had to take an **entrance exam**.
Well, not just take it, you had to **pass it**.
Well, **not just** pass it, you had to **totally ace it.**

I totally aced it.

It's an incredible school,
backed by a lot of big-money types
like **Wilson Fisk** and **Alchemax Laboratories.**

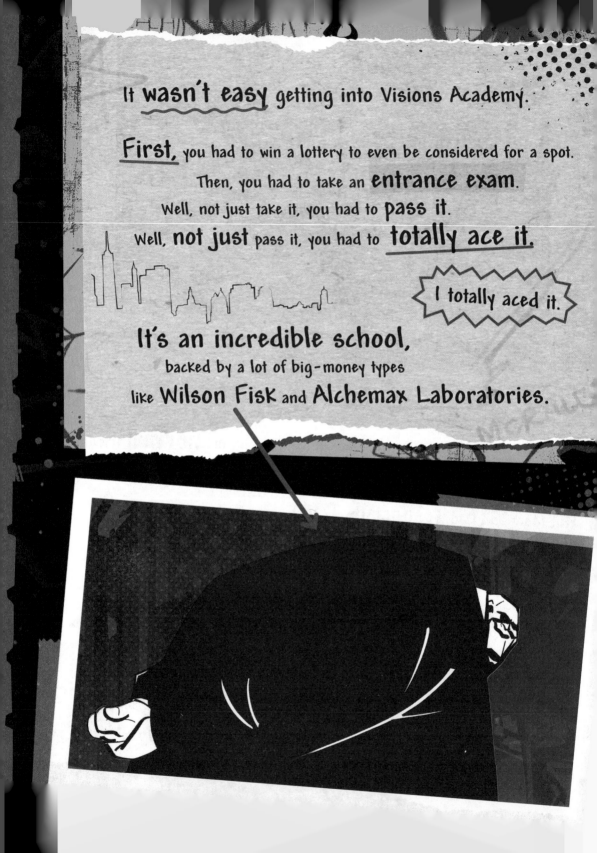

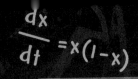

$$\frac{dx}{dt} = x(1-x)$$

$$V_2 = V_1 \frac{A_1}{A_2}$$

This is Ms. Calleros, one of my teachers.

PHYSICS.

...e's **super smart**

...d **super intimidating,**

...d I'm always **super late**

...ner class. I had to write down

...s conversation we had

...other day, because

...ought it was funny:

LOL

Ms. CALLEROS: **You're late**, Mr. Morales.

ME: Einstein said time was **relative**, right? Maybe **I'm not late.** Maybe **you guys are early.**

...uess who didn't laugh?

...ight—Ms. Calleros.

I've got to learn not to talk so much and just do physics.

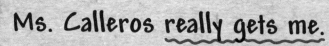

Ms. Calleros really gets me.

She **knows** that I'm having a hard time adjusting to the new s...
and that **I sort of don't really want to be her** ...
even though **I'm trying.**

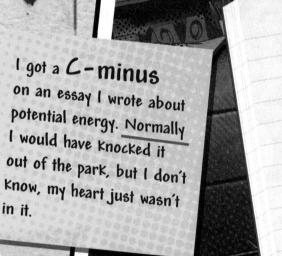

I got a **C-minus** on an essay I wrote about potential energy. Normally I would have knocked it out of the park, but I don't know, my heart just wasn't in it.

$C-$

Potential Energy Essay

Miles Morales

$$P.E. = m \times g \times h$$

m: mass
g: Gravitational Accel...
h: Height   (9.8 m/s...

Ms. Calleros was cool, though.
She let me rewrite the essay.
Need more teachers like her.

MILES

One pretty <u>awesome thing</u> we watched in Ms. Calleros's class was a documentary on Multiverse Theory.

...director of Alchemax Laboratories ...trying to explain the thinking ...nd it, and I was <u>fascinated.</u> ...so sure about the other kids in class.

...re on this later, because I have ...eeling it's going to be huge.

$z \cdot f_p \cdot n_e \cdot f_l \cdot f_i \cdot f_c \cdot L$

I think one of the **biggest** changes of going to Visions is actually living on campus.

MY BEDROOM.

Work is life now!

When I went to Brooklyn Middle, it was just like any other school— y'know, you went to class and you came home.

Here, we go to class and then we go back to our **dorms.**

My room is okay, I guess.

Even if I do have a roommate who doesn't really talk to me.

So if I don't want to **not talk** to my roommate and I don't have class, I can always take advantage of one of the lab spaces.

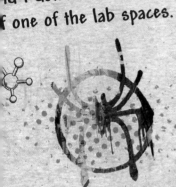

hey're really igh-tech,

ke something out of a movie.

Every kind of equipment you could ask for!

It's like playing with the **world's biggest**, best **LEGO** set.

I wonder what I might come up with in a place like this!

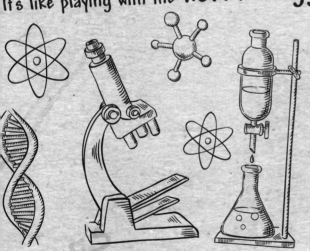

Or what kind of trouble
I might get into...!

One thing I remember my mom telling me about before my first day at Visions was the reading.

"There might be a little more reading than you'd usually have at Brooklyn Middle,"

she said.

Man, she wasn't joking

First day there, I got hit! **Book** after **book** and at least a chapter from each every night.

(And) we have to remember it all!

I'm still getting used to the place, but it's starting to grow on me.

I may not have a bunch of friends like I used to at Brooklyn Middle, but I'm **happy** for the **good friends** I am making.

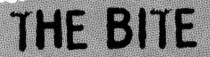

THE BITE

SPIDEY!

AAAAHHHHH!!!!!

In case you wondered, THAT'S the sound I made when I was bitten by a weird glowing spider!

That night totally **changed my life.**

I'm going write it all down, so I don't forget.

Not that I ever could.

I was **so busy** painting with Uncle Aaron,
I didn't even notice the spider.
I was in the zone.
Just listening to music,
I was lost in the art.
Guess that spider was lost, too.

Something had happened to it. The way it was glowing...
If I had seen it, I'm **sure** I would have jumped
and none of this would have ever happened.

But I didn't see it.

But it...

saw me.

I **freaked out** when the thing bit me. I felt kind of **weird** after. Started sweating a lot, for one thing. When I got back to the dorms that night, I jumped into bed and passed out.

But when I woke up in the morning, that's when I really started to notice that something was different. Like, my school uniform was too short. I tho

Miles, did you shrink your school uniform?

But then I remembered that I don't do my own laundry precisely so I __DON'T__ accidentally shrink anything. So then I thought,

Miles, are you going through puberty?

But that wasn't it, either.

That's weird...
My school
uniform shrank.

So far, so weird. Then I ran into Wanda.

I already told you about this.

Put my hand on her shoulder,
stuck to her, blah blah blah.

But you know how it is.
You're a kid, you've got a lot on your mind,

you're busy sticking to people.

Oh, and remember the security guard,
the one whose office I ran into by accident?

Well, he was chasing me, so I got into his office and slammed the doo

Next thing I knew, I found myself sticking to EVERYTH

Even the **walls!**

I started to go ria

Good thing I rolled out the
window **before** anyone saw me.

Not that I <u>INTENDED</u> to roll out the window.

hat night, I went back down to the subway tunnel, to find the spider.

Sure enough, it was glowing.
I don't know if you know this or not, but spiders don't usually glow.
Like, ever.

MILES

Things got even stranger when I looked down an abandoned tunnel and saw the word ALCHEMAX stamped on it. Not sure what business they would have messing around in the subway tunnels. But I didn't have any time to think about it. I had this really uneasy feeling, like something was telling me to **MOVE IT!** So I did and a second later, a subway car smashed right into the wall.

I think that **uneasy** feeling was warning me of danger.
I must've got it from the spider!

Along with some crazy reflexes that let me jump out of the way.

Things were moving **SO** fast that it took
a minute to register what was going on.

There I was, caught between **Spider-Man**
and the **Green Goblin**—on a school night!

Never in a **million years** did
I think **I'd** ever meet Spider-Man.

I think that's when it really hit me—I had spider powers,
too, just like him! Well, maybe not JUST like him.

But probably just **like** him.

Y'know, I don't know.

Spidey said something about some of the other Spider-People or whatever being able to generate their own webbing.

THWIP!

He can't, so he made these web-shooters that he wears on his wrists.

I got to use 'em, too.

All you have to do is tap the button in the middle of your palm and THWIP!

SPIDER-MAN

Instant web.

Let's see, what else can I do? Oh yeah,

venom strikes!

That's what I call them, anyway. One of the powers I picked up from the spider bite. All I have to do is raise my hands and **WHAM!**

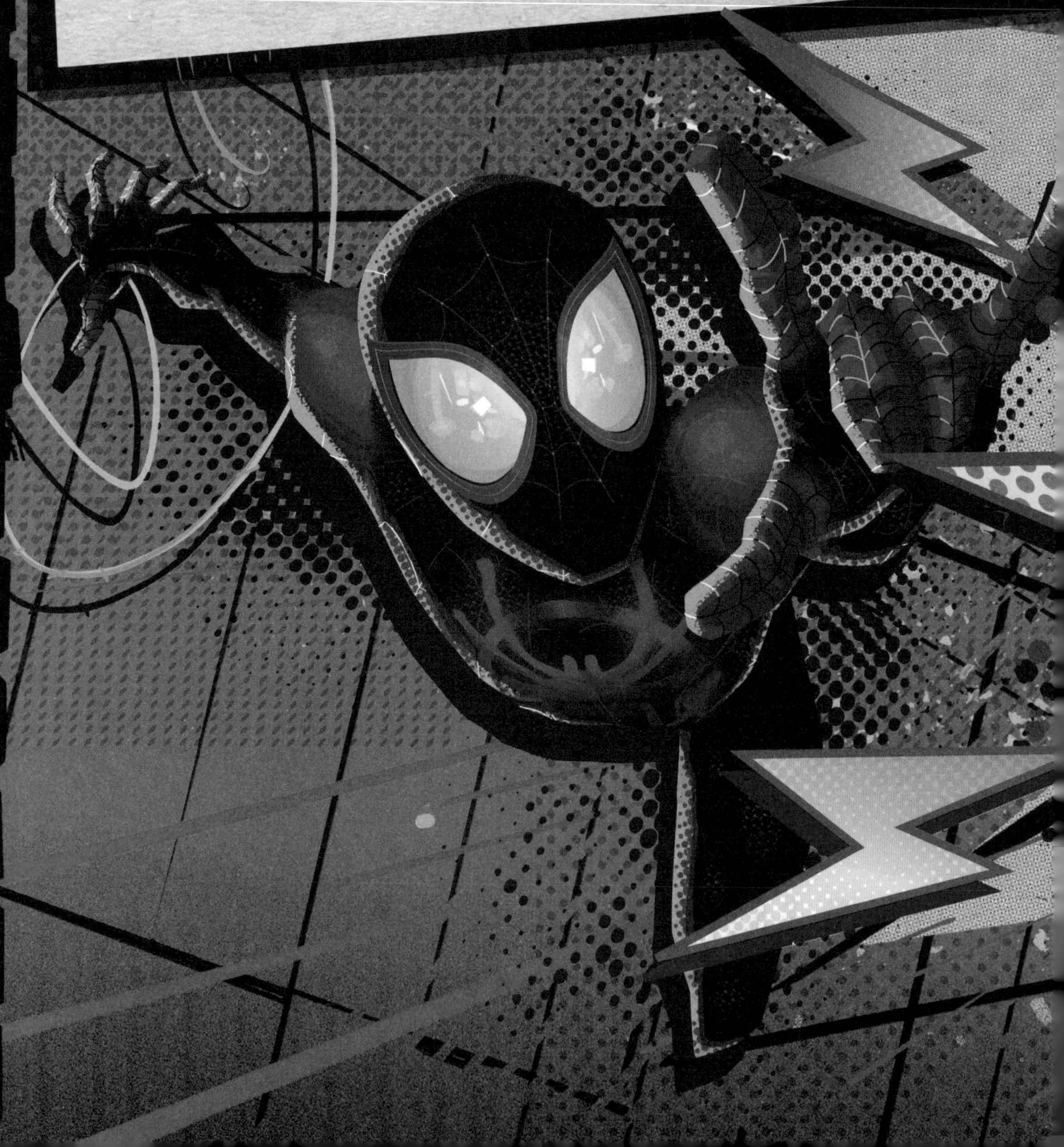

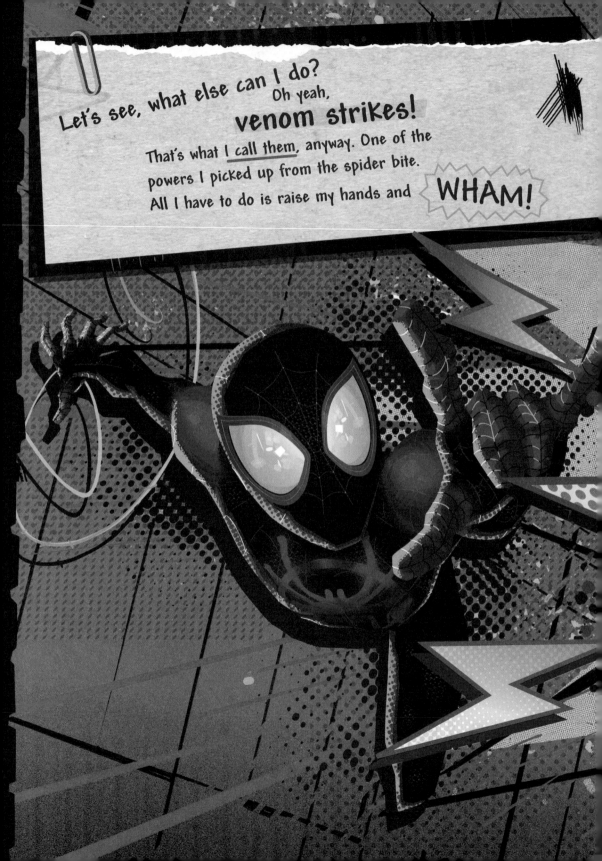

There's probably more to it than that, **biologically speaking,** but that's essentially what happens.

If I hit someone, they're pretty much out of it for a while.

It's going to take <u>some time</u> to get used to this.

One thing I did figure out right away was that I was going to need a **costume**. Sure, there was the classic Spider-Man look.

But maybe I could try something **different...**

something **bold ...**

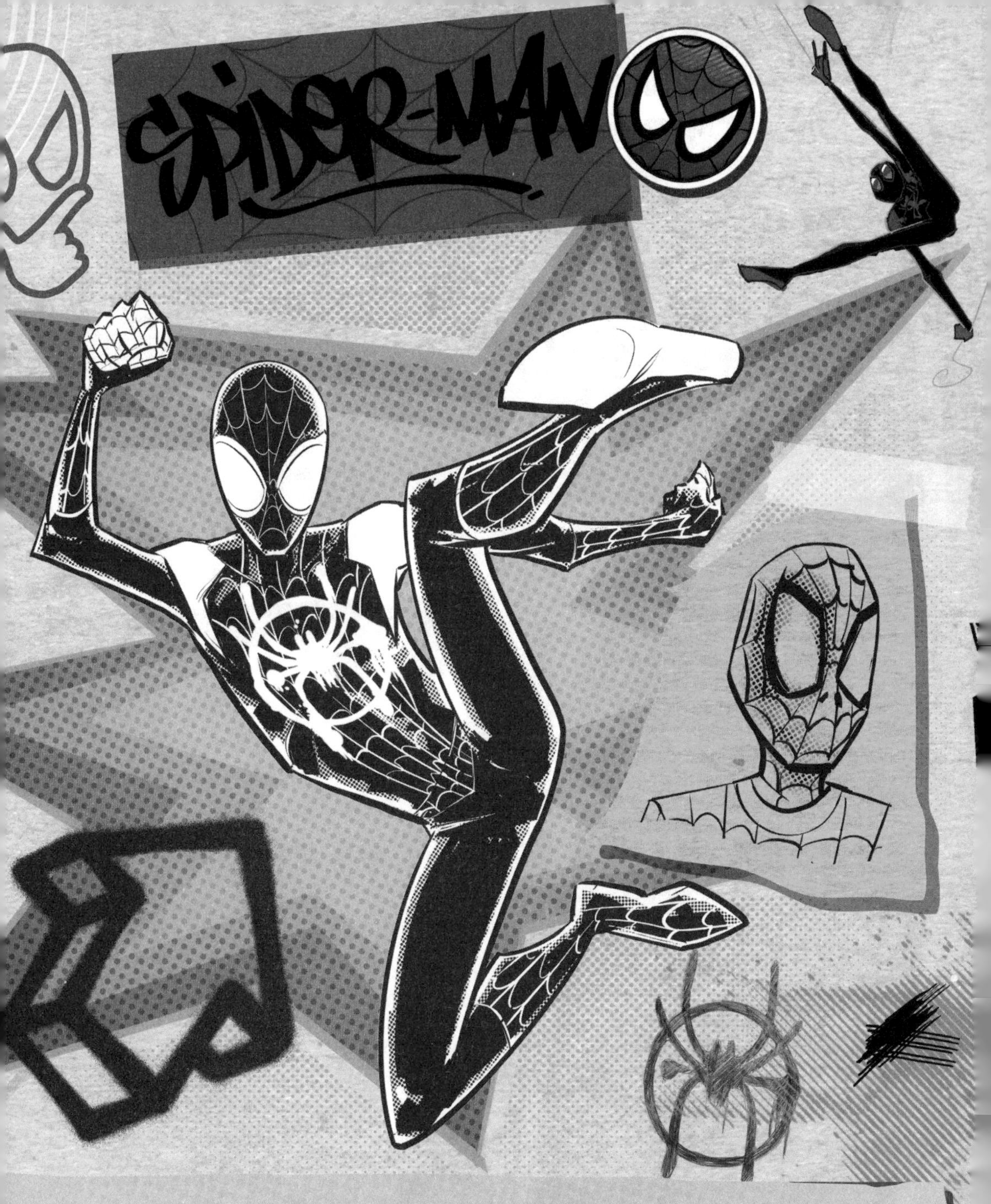
SPIDER-MAN

omething **daring!**

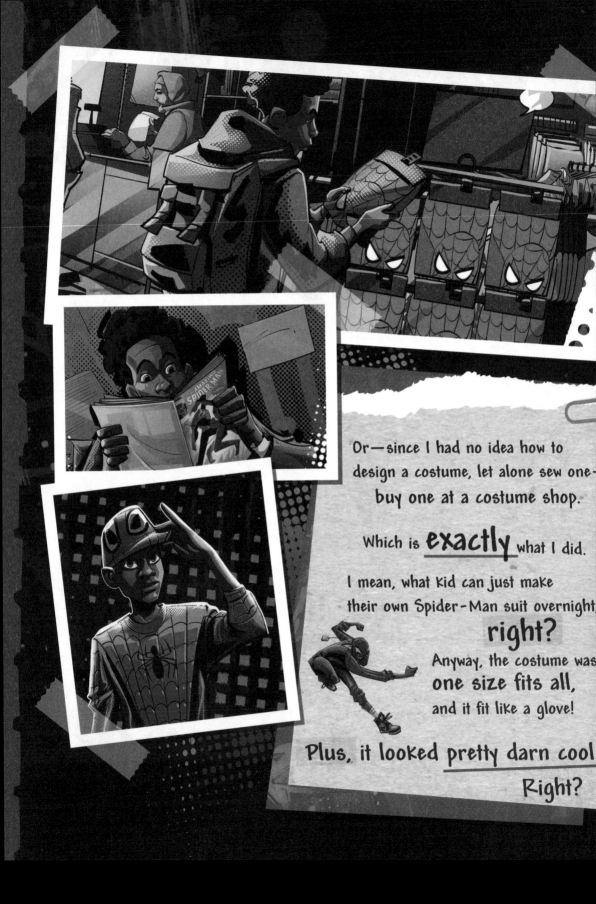

Or—since I had no idea how to design a costume, let alone sew one—buy one at a costume shop.

Which is **exactly** what I did.

I mean, what kid can just make their own Spider-Man suit overnight, **right?**

Anyway, the costume was **one size fits all,** and it fit like a glove!

Plus, it looked pretty darn cool

Right?

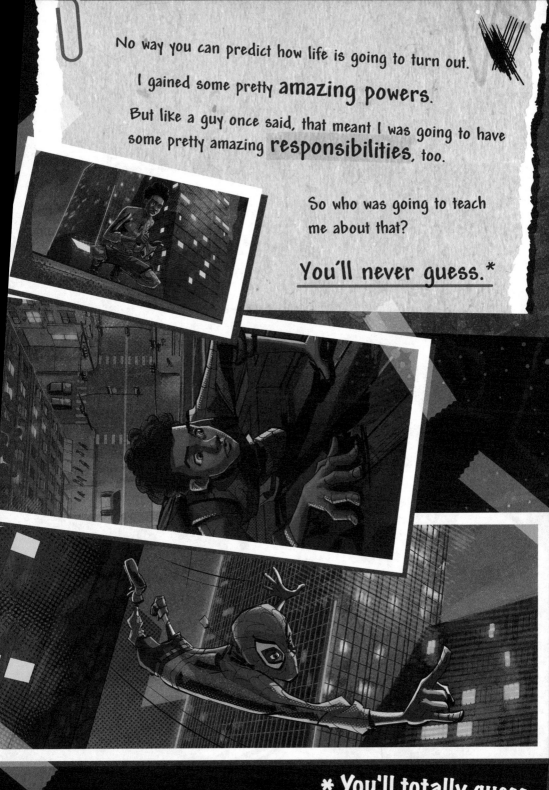

No way you can predict how life is going to turn out.

I gained some pretty **amazing powers**.

But like a guy once said, that meant I was going to have some pretty amazing **responsibilities**, too.

So who was going to teach me about that?

You'll never guess.*

*** You'll totally guess.**

PETER PARKER(S)

Spider-Man is really **Peter Parker.**

Actually, there's more than one Spider-Man.

And more than one Peter Parker.

Boy, this really is (confusing.)

Let me try to explain it all as clearly as I can. Because I'm not sure that even I understand it!

The first Spider-Man I met
was a guy named Peter Parker.

He was older than me,
but not, like, **really old**.

Maybe, like, 27 or so.

He was fighting

the Green Goblin,

a 25-foot-tall dude
with wings.

Peter knew he had to stop
the Goblin and he did.

Peter was the first one who knew **exactly**

what had happened to me
and what I had become.

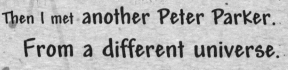

Then I met **another Peter Parker.**
From a different universe.
But more on that later.

This Peter Parker was older
than the first one I met.

He was also Spider-Man.

He'd been doing that job
for years in his own universe,
before he got sucked into some
crazy, psychedelic portal
and arrived in <u>my world</u>.

Peter knew all the
ins and outs
of being a Super Hero.

So if anyone could teach me
how to be a wall-crawling,
web-slinging good guy,
it was **definitely him.**

At first I couldn't work out **why**
ere were **two Peter Parkers.**

So I did what you do
when you don't know what's going on.

u tie a guy to a chair and **get some answers.**

Peter told me what he thought was going on,
and I **totally** guessed that he came from a different universe.

Go, me!

I asked Peter to teach me how to be Spider-Man
and he agreed. He had a whole bunch of lessons.

First lesson?

"Don't watch the mouth. Watch the hands."

Turns out the whole time I was listening to Peter talk, he was busy untying himself. Got to remember that one.

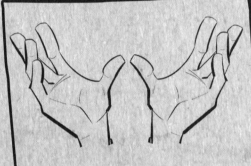

DON'T WATCH

WATCH

 ## Second lesson?

"Don't be a fool, stay in school."

This he told me right after he kicked a chair at me and webbed my mouth shut. Turns out, he didn't really want to help me learn to be Spider-Man. He just wanted to get back to his own universe.

Then he tried to leave, but **something happened**.

It was like he glitched—

like his body didn't like being away from his own universe.

Here I was, thinking that Peter Parker could **teach** me. It turned out he was a **terrible** teacher! But I **still** needed his help.

A bad guy called the Kingpin had developed this supercollider. He'd already used it at least once, and Peter was pretty sure that's what opened the portal that brought him to my world. But it also caused a **massive** earthquake here.

If the Kingpin used it again, it would **destroy** Brooklyn. Bye-bye, Mom; bye-bye, Dad; bye-bye, EVERYONE.

It took a lot, but I **finally** convinced Peter to stay. Even if he kind of thought that it was his own idea.

I guess the third lesson was,

"Watch Peter eat before doing anything else

REALLY?!?

It turned out that in Peter's universe, this burger joint had closed six years ago. So he insisted on getting a burger before any further lessons. Here are a couple of pro tips he gave me in between bites:

* Disinfect the mask
* Put baby powder in the suit to avoid <u>chafing</u>

Yeah, he was a baaaaaaad teac

But I'd started to come around. had this insane idea that I would wear a yellow cape with my costume.

L.O.L

thought it looked cool.

In retrospect, I'm sure it didn't.

(But Peter?)

knew it looked awful right away. "It's a **no** on the **cape!**" he said, and he **yanked** it right off.

Then he blew his nose on it.

SPIDER-MAN

I had a lot to learn about being Spider-Man, **apparently.**

Even though I thought that this Peter Parker wasn't **the best**, it turned out that he really could teach me a lot. Like how to remain **calm** under pressure. We were hacking into Alchemax's computer mainframe when the Kingpin showed up. Instead of **freaking out** (like I was doing!), Peter was cool as a cucumber. ➞

We kept a low profile, got what we needed, then we were **out of there.**

And **the**
I learned that I could
invisibl

"I'm invisible!
Get it?"

A LESSON PETER
DID NOT TEACH ME

was a **bumpy ride,**
the more I hung out with Peter,
more I realized that he had the
der-Man thing **down**.

I was all concerned about learning how
to crawl up walls and swing on webs.

But he taught me that there's other stuff that's just as important—

maybe **more important**.

Because it doesn't matter what powers you've got.*

What matters is what do you do with 'em.

*Okay, it matters a little.

Multiverse Theory and You!

I'm still trying to wrap my head around Multiverse Theory.
It's kind of mind-blowing!

If you sit down and try to explain it to somebody (like Mom), they sort of look at you like you have four extra arms or something.

But I think if I writ it all down, it'll star to make some sens

At least, I hope it w

We watched this documentary about Multiverse Theory in Ms. Calleros's class. The director of Alchemax Laboratories explained it kind of like this:

Every choice we make could create <u>countless</u> other possibilities, a "What If" to infinity. That's the Multiverse.

Huh?

Okay, what I think it really means is this....

Say you're making an important decision, like what to have for breakfast.

Pick one:

 CEREAL BACON AND EGGS

Congratulations! There are now TWO realities:

One where you had cereal for breakfast. One where you had bacon and eggs. So somewhere out there, different worlds—universes—exist, similar to our own, but with <u>many, many</u> differences.

Or, to put it another way, here's what I said when I tried to figure out how I could **possibly** meet <u>**two Peter Parkers:**</u>

"Are you from **another** dimension? Like a parallel universe where things are like this universe, but different? And you're Spider-Man in that universe and you somehow traveled to this universe?"

Peter **KNEW** what I was talking about.

Of course he <u>**KNEW**</u> what I was talking about.

He's
<u>Spider-Man!</u>

Just so you can see, this is my brain.

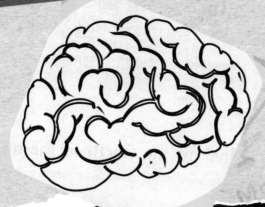

This is my brain on Multiverse Theory.

BOOOM

IT'S NUTS.

I drew this the other night when I couldn't sleep

Sometimes it helps to have a **visual** in front of you.
Looking at this makes Multiverse Theory easy to understand.

I live on the Earth in the midd

Branching out from it
are all the other Earths,
each with a different
Spider-Man.

I've already met a ton of them and I'll write about 'em later.

But how do you go from **one world** to **another?**

It's not like you can just open a door and walk through.

Or can you?

The Kingpin thinks so. He forced scientists to build a supercollider that could harness energy and open a rift between parallel worlds, allowing things to move back and forth between them.

If it sounds messy and dangerous, that's because it is.

I think I mentioned the earthquakes it caused before. **Bad stuff.**

Turns out there are some physical side effects to moving between worlds, too.

Peter experienced them right after he came to my world. He'd be fine one minute, then ZAP! His powers would cut out and he'd fall, then he'd quickly recover.

I call it glitching.

Or as Peter put it,
"I don't think my atoms are real jazzed about being in the wrong dimension."

Scrambled atoms aside,

it really makes you stop to thin[k]

...le you're doing something in your world, at that **exact moment** something similar but completely different could be happening to "you" in countless other worlds.

Since I met Peter(s),
I've met a few Spiders from different worl

One of those worlds I call Earth-14512.
(yeah, I numbered 'em—makes it easier to keep track of it all.)

On that one, there's no Spider-Man like I know.

It's kind of a robot, called SP//dr,
and a kid named Peni Parker.

And then there's Earth-90214.

It's a pretty strange place—the world is actually **black and white!**

I'm _not_ talking about the morality. I'm talking about the _color_—

literally **everything** is shades of black and white.

Not sure how the science
of all that works.

I should ask Ms. Calleros
sometime....

Last but not least, there's Earth-8311.

I don't even know <u>where</u> to begin.

The Spider-Man from that world is a...

well, <u>he's a pig.</u>

But not like a run-around-on-all-fours pig.

You Know what? I'll explain later.

<u>Anyway,</u>

that world is about as different from mine as you can **possibly** get.

Spiders! SPIDERS! SPIDERS!!!!!!!!!!

I added lots of exclamation marks because I thought it would make this page seem really exciting. It kind of does. **So yeah, Spiders!**

There sure are a lot of them. At first, like everyone else, I thought there was just the one Spider-Man. But I was proven wrong **pretty quickly.** Not only did I meet a second Spider-Man, but then I started to meet different Spider-People from different worlds.

And not only people—**pigs!**

A talking pig! **Freaky!**

Yeah, so...a talking pig.

It took a little getting used to,
y'know, having a conversation with a hog.
But Spider-Ham (can't believe I have to call him that)
is just as heroic as the other Spiders.
Turns out, he has a pretty strange origin.

He used to be a plain, ordinary spider
who was bitten by a radioactive pig.

The bite transformed that little spider into an awesome pig with
spider powers, who decided to put on a costume and fight crime.

He's got a little bit of an attitude, but I kind of like that.
I'm a Brooklyn kid; we all have attitude!

Spider-Gwen's about as different from a talking pig as you can get. She's **really** a kid named **Gwen Stacy** and she's **15**—not much older than me.

She got her **spider powers** from the bite of a radioactive spider.

(I see a theme developing....)

In her world, Peter Parker turned into some kind of **lizard creature** or something?

Oh, and she's a dead ringer for **Wanda!**
Man, this Multiverse stuff is a trip.

Now, THIS guy is serious.

Sooooooo serious.

Makes me glad we had a talking pig around to lighten the mood.

I already told you a little about his world, all black and white?

Yeah, weird.

Anyway.

He was bitten by a **non**-radioactive spider that came out of an antique spider statue.

creepy.

The bite gave him what I call

the standard Spider-Man powers.

Then he used them to fight the Goblin in his world, as well as a creepy dude called the Vulture.

Okay,

ow this kid's cool!

ni was bitten by a radioactive spider, but she didn't get

standard Spider-Man powers.

Instead, the spider bite
forged a bond
between her and the spider.

nd together, they are able to pilot
omething called the SP//dr suit—
kind of robot Spider-Man (it even has web-shooters!) made by her father.

That SP//dr can do all the stuff that the Spider-People can do.

Plus, IT'S A ROBOT.

Now, you may think that hanging out with a whole bunch of Spider-People (and pig) would be **awesome**. And you'd be right!

SPIDER-MAN (PETER PARKER): Cracking jokes while fighting helps you relax. But avoid the potty humor. You're better than that.

SPIDER-GWEN: You n to learn about maintainir control of your abilities.

SPIDER-MAN NOIR: Punch, punch, kick, punch, head fake, head fake, head fake...

But the one thing you wouldn't think is that each one of 'em would have advice for a young-and-impressionable new Spider-Man (me).

They had no problem giving it to me, either,

and all at the same time.

Too bad that spider bite didn't give me spider hearing!*

SPIDER-HAM:
Disinfect the mask.
Trust me. I'm a pig.

PENI PARKER: Let me tell you a thing or thirty about electrical engineering...

*Is that a thing?
...ot sure if that's a thing.
Probably not a thing.

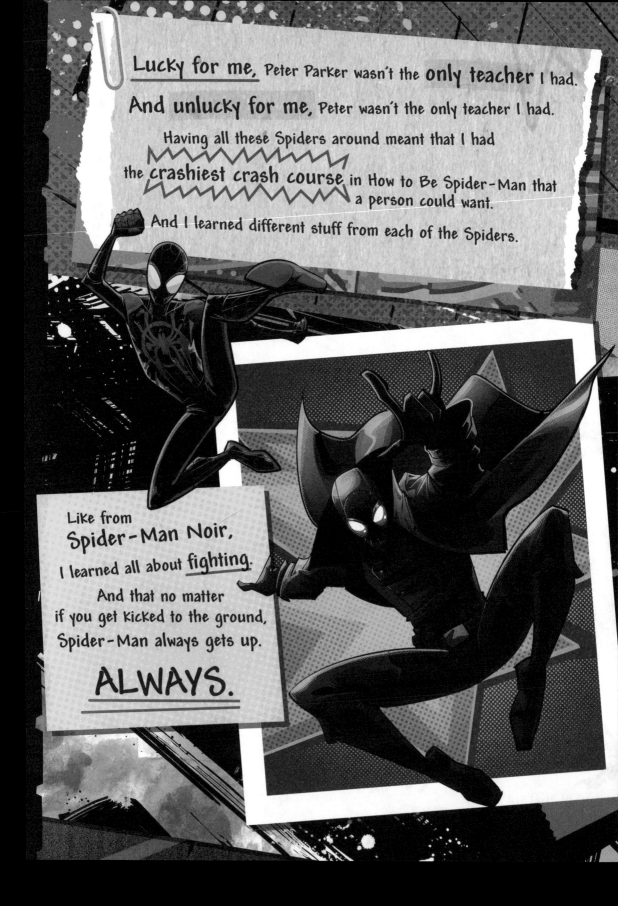

Lucky for me, Peter Parker wasn't the **only teacher** I had.

And unlucky for me, Peter wasn't the only teacher I had.

Having all these Spiders around meant that I had the **crashiest crash course** in How to Be Spider-Man that a person could want.

And I learned different stuff from each of the Spiders.

Like from **Spider-Man Noir,** I learned all about **fighting.**

And that no matter if you get kicked to the ground, Spider-Man always gets up.

ALWAYS.

And even though Peter likes to joke around (which isn't always funny), he had some **really** <u>good</u> advice for me.

He said,

"**Every** Spider-Person in **every** dimension has faced a test,
and we've all come through.
You can't just run away when it gets hard."

Sometimes I wish I could just run away. But I know Peter's right.
Spider-Man <u>can't just quit</u>. He <u>has</u> to be there.
<u>Especially</u> when it counts. <u>Because it always counts.</u>

I had, like, **eight hours** to learn how to be Spider-Man.
All these other Spiders had **years**.

But I had something they didn't have—**them**.

I got a little something from each one,
and after a while, something just... clicked

It's like I got

And maybe it's because we're **all** Spiders, we're all linked through the Multiverse, but <u>we</u> just clicked, too.

Bring us together...
there's no telling what we can do!

Well, I'll tell you one thing we could do. We were having a **big** meeting in my dorm room, and Ganke walked in on us.

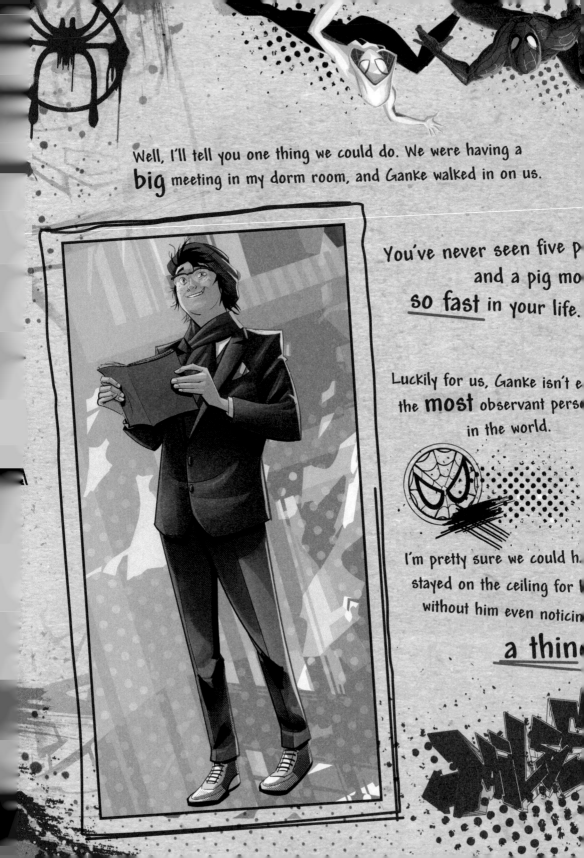

You've never seen five p
and a pig mo
so fast in your life.

Luckily for us, Ganke isn't e
the **most** observant perse
in the world.

I'm pretty sure we could h
stayed on the ceiling for
without him even noticin

a thing

SUPER VILLAINS?
More Like Super Annoyance

Someone told me there's an old saying, that a hero is only as good as their villain.

wish that saying wasn't true, because it would mean that I get hit **a lot** less.
I've only been Spider-Man for a little while,
but I've already faced off against some pretty **tough** Super Villains.

First up are your garden-variety baddies. **Just punks**, really.
Guys who lend their muscle to make money.
In this town, most of these jerks work for the Kingpin.
They don't have any powers—
like, they're not going to shoot blasts out of their eyes
or paralyze anyone with a six-foot-long poison tongue.
But they _do_ make things more difficult
and can wear you down before you face off
against one of the **REALLY bad guys**

I have a few tips on taking down punks, which,
strangely enough, spell out the word

PUNK:

P – Put 'em down fast!
U – Unless you don't have to!
N – Never go overboard!
K – Kick back and relax when you've finished

Okay, I admit it. I just made that up for the journal

Okay, now I would put this guy in the punk class, except he's a **step above a punk**. I don't know what the word is for that, but he's definitely it.

This guy works for the **Kingpin** and will do **anything** he asks, without question. He's got pasty-white skin and **creepy pointed teeth**. Super strong, **Tombstone** can also take a beating— like, I've seen Spider-Man punch him right in the face and it's as though that guy **doesn't even feel it.**

The Scorpion is another guy who's kind of like a punk, but isn't a punk, because he's got some serious powers.

Like Tombstone, he works for **the Kingpin.**

Unlike Tombstone, he has a set of **scorpion-like powers** (I guess that accounts for the name)—mainly **super strength**

He wears a heavy-duty suit of armor with a tail attached to it.

That tail is deadly!

It can smash stuff and it can spray acid, too

Pretty sure a regular scorpion **can't** do that, but what do I know?*

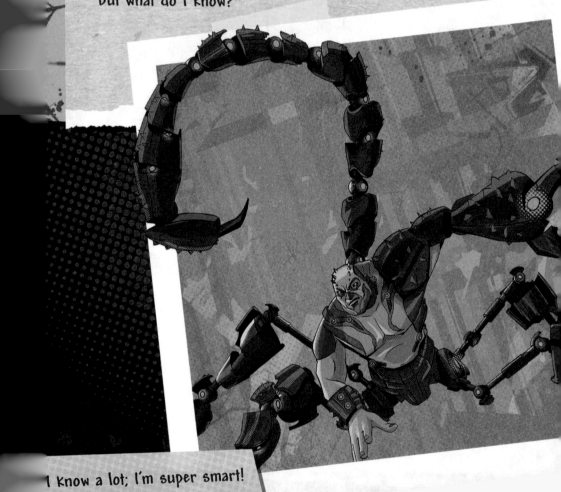

I know a lot; I'm super smart!

Q: Is every villain in this city employed by the Kingpin?

A: **Yes!**

Well, maybe not **every** villain, but it sure seems that way.

The Green Goblin also worked for the Kingpin,
 but it's pretty hard to imagine that a guy
 like that would work for **anybody**.

First of all, the Goblin had to be about **25 feet tall**, easy.

On his back, he had these **two huge wings** and he could flap
'em and fly anywhere. And he had this crazy-long blue tongue.

Did I mention that he was super strong, too?
Yeah, he was **super strong**, too.

I never had to fight him. I watched Spider-Man*
take him on, though. He nearly beat the web-head.
Ugh, the less I think about that the better.

*The first Peter Parker I met, not the second one.

The Prowler not only works for the Kingpin (surprise!),
but he's also kind of like his **right-hand man.**
Also his left-hand man. Maybe even his feet, too.
The Prowler is like the go-to guy,
the one who can always get the job done.
Of course, **every job** is a dirty one for this guy.
He's really strong and the **gauntlets** he wears
can **blast** unsuspecting Spiders.

And here we have the **ultimate bad guy**, the main man who's in charge of all that's wrong in New York City.

The Kingpin. His real name is Wilson Fisk, the man behind Fisk Industries, one of the most powerful corporations **in the world.**

Most people think Fisk is just a rich dude who donates money to hospitals and zoos.* But the few heroes who have uncovered his real identity know that Fisk controls almost **all the crime in New York.**

Which doesn't explain why he's using a supercollider to bridge the gap between the different worlds in the Multiverse.

What's his game?
Why is he doing it? Only the Kingpin **knows...**
but I'm going to find out.

*I don't know for sure if he donates money to zoos. That's just a guess.

Just wanted to write down a **few** observations on each of these bad guys

Not like I won't remember them forever!

TOMBSTONE

Knows how to throw a punch.
Hurts when you hit his skin—
it's hard!
Nice hair, though.

SCORPION

Watch out for the tail.
Repeat—watch out for the tail!
Acid = no fun.

GREEN GOBLIN

Tongue = gross!
How'd he get so tall?

PROWLER

Costume looks cool, for a bad guy.
Seems really familiar...
do I know him?

THE KINGPIN

For someone **so big,**
he moves really fast!
And he knows how to hit!

I still can't believe everything that's happened to me.

I went from **zero** to battling **Super Villains** in one day.

From never having been in a fight in my life to fighting **for my life.**

It all seems like a **dream** sometimes...

or a pretty nasty nightmare!

And I can't believe I'm at the end of this journal **already**

when my career as Spider-Man has only **just started!**

I'll have to get another notebook
so I can keep writing.

have no idea

what the future holds,

ut I'm **sure** of one thing—

won't be boring!

	MONDAY	TUESDAY	WEDNES
7:30-9:00 AM	Social Studies	Introduction to Literature	Social Stud
9:05-10:25 AM	Trigonometry	Computer Science	Trigonome
10:30-11:25 AM	Advanced Physics	Study Hall	Advance Physics
11:30 AM-12:00 PM	Lunch	Lunch	Lunch
12:05-1:30 PM	Anatomy & Physiology	Physical Education	Anatomy Physiolog
1:35-3:00 PM	History	Advanced Physics Lab	History
4:00 PM-12:00 AM			STUDY
12:00-7:25 AM	Sleep?	Sleep would be good	Seriously, s

VISIONS

URSDAY	FRIDAY
troduction Literature	Social Studies
uter Science	Trigonometry
tudy Hall	Advanced Physics
Lunch	Lunch
cal Education	Anatomy & Physiology
nced Physics Lab	History
EEEEEEP!	Zzzzzzzzzzzzzz

Here's my class schedule at BVA. MOST. EXCITING. READING MATERIAL. EVER!!! Seriously, how am I supposed to concentrate on class now that I'm, you know, SPIDER-MAN?!

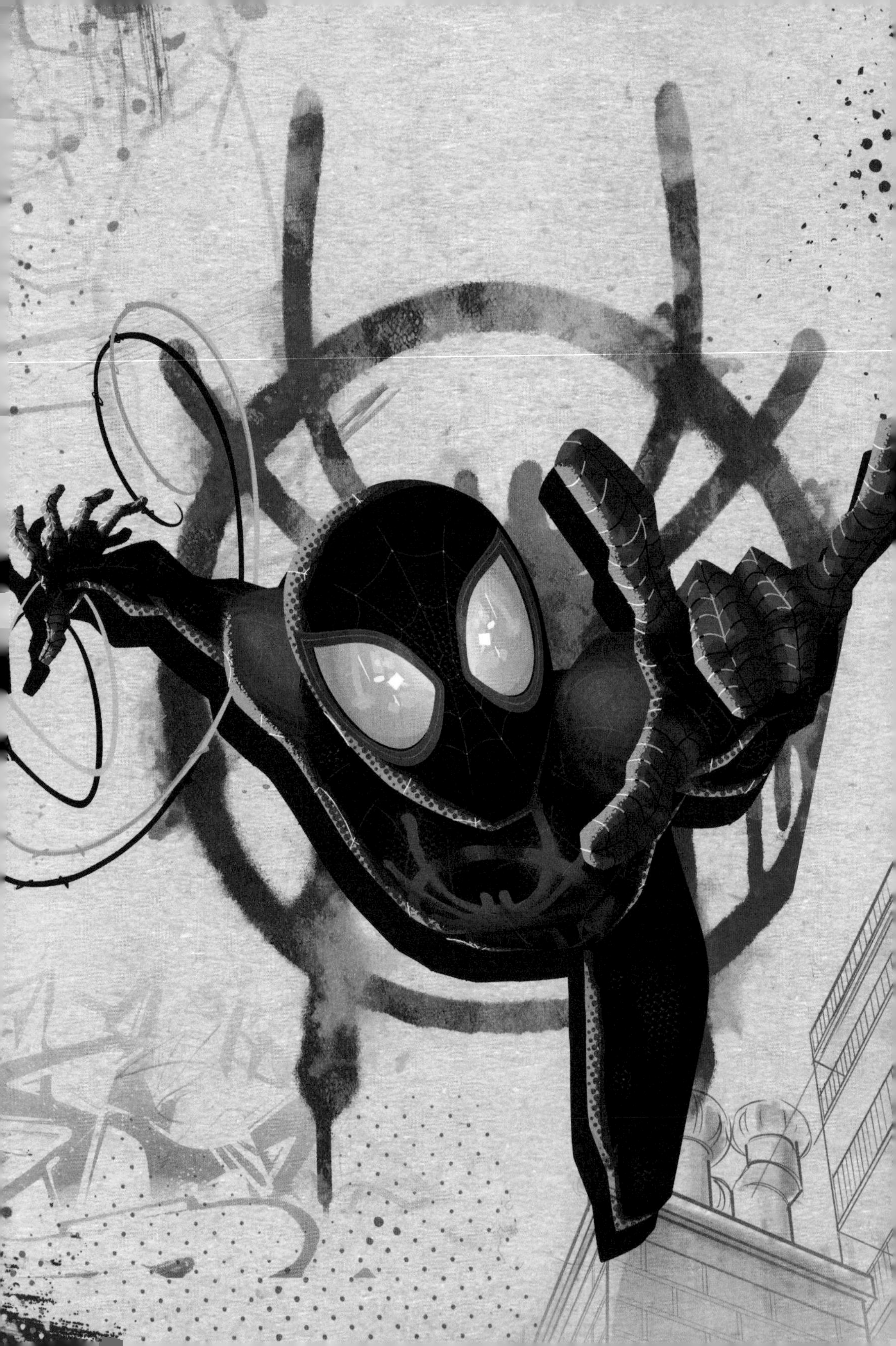

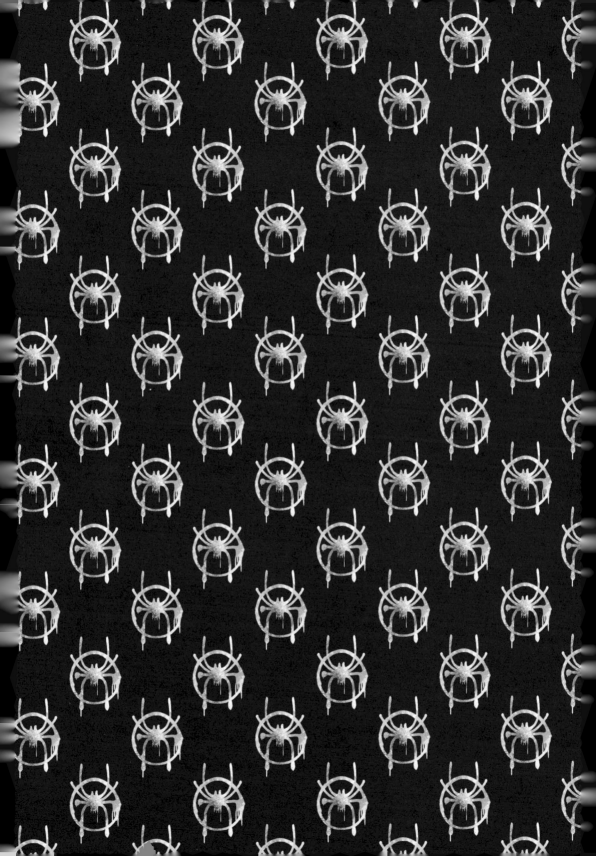

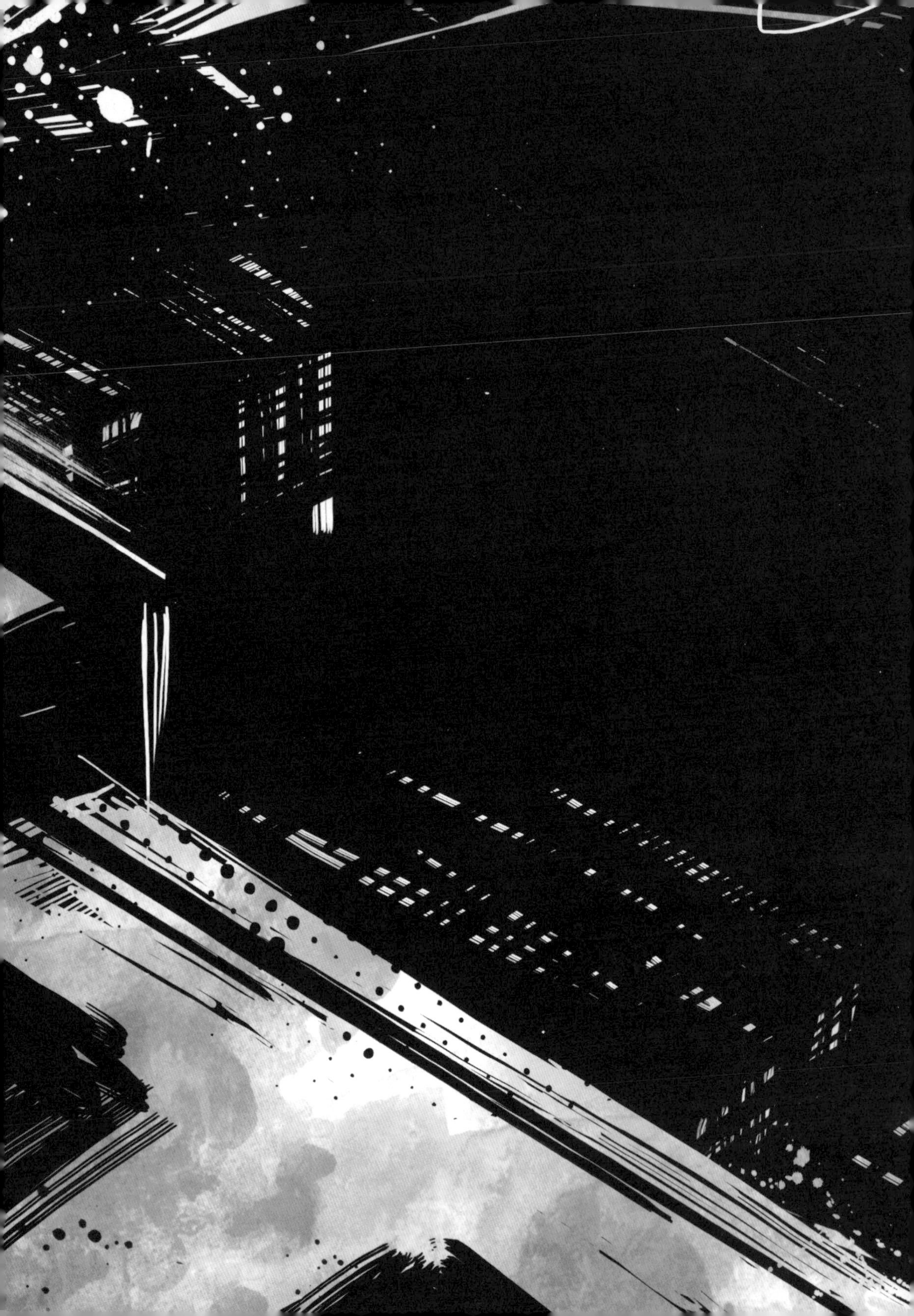